T0380910

OPILOPY

ELLIOTT ALTER

Archway Publishing books may be ordered through booksellers or by contacting:

Archway Publishing
1663 Liberty Drive
Bloomington, IN 47403
www.archwaypublishing.com
844-669-3957

ISBN: 978-1-6657-6160-4 (sc)
ISBN: 978-1-6657-6161-1 (e)

Library of Congress Control Number: 2024912214

Print information available on the last page.

Archway Publishing rev. date: 07/05/2024

Somewhere between Polaris and the Limpopo River is a magical land of adventures, courage, kindness, friendship, and team work.

This magical land is OPILOPY and it's waiting for you.

"What's all the racket?" I jolted awake.

I recognized voices from everyone in my family: grandparents, parents, aunts, uncles, and cousins.

I threw on my clothes and ran to the living room where it seemed everyone had already started a celebration without me. And at a very early hour.

"What's everyone doing here?" I asked "Ashley, we want to take you to the harbor, where an enchanted ship is waiting to take you on a magical adventure with lessons to learn." Said my father.

"Do I have to go by myself?" I whispered.

"We all went on the same adventure the first day of summer on our tenth year." My mother said with a reassuring hand on my shoulder.

Overhearing my timid squeak to my mother, "Of course not Ashley'" boomed the deep voice of my uncle. "Children from all around the city and some of your neighborhood friends will go with you. On the summer solstice of your tenth year every child travels on a magical adventure.

"Is this for real?" I wondered out loud. Everyone chuckled and gave me big smiles and nods.

I quickly packed up a bag and with everyone in my family, headed to the harbor.

There, tied to the dock was the most beautiful ship I had ever seen. With tall colorful flags and intricately carved wooden railings, polished to a lustrous sheen.

My friends and I were all talking at the same time when we heard a loud roar come from the top of the gangway. An enormous lion came into view and bellowed, "Are these the children?" I had never seen a lion before outside of a zoo much less a talking lion and was too nervous to say anything.

"Yes!" The adults answered in unison.

"Then our journey begins now." Said the lion a bit softer.

With that, all the children said goodbye to their parents and followed the lion up into the ship and down to the mess.

There was a large wooden table with long benches where we were told to sit for our meal. Once we were all seated, very tall, walking, and talking grasshoppers, dressed up in tuxedos brought out trays of food. We couldn't believe our eyes. There was so much food: toast and jam, eggs and bacon, pies, cookies, and cake. We ate until we had our fill.

One of the children suggested we go upstairs and look at the ocean.

5

The lion was standing by the ship's wheel making sure we were headed in the right direction. The sky was cloudy and it looked as if it might rain. Suddenly, the lion gave the biggest roar I had ever heard. The clouds went away, the sun appeared, and dove after dove flew down to land on the railings. Up ahead we saw an enormous island.

"Where are we?" My friend Markus asked the lion.

"Why, you are at the land of Opilopy! The lion said with a smile.

We had never heard of such a place. I looked down into the water to see the ripples the boat was making, and there, right below was a beautiful mermaid. With a shiny green tail and long golden hair, she smiled and waved until I gathered my wits and waved back.

Soon the ship stopped and a plank was lowered to let us walk onto the island.

As we wandered about, we came upon a giant stone door partially hidden by vines on the side of a very large hill. The door was engraved with pirates, mermaids, and creatures I couldn't wait to discover. The lion walked close to the door, whispered a magical phrase that we could not understand, and the big mighty door opened.

The lion then turned toward us. "I will go back and stay on the ship. It is up to you to be courageous and discover the island on your own." The lion said calmly.

I looked around to see everyone's eyes as big as mine felt.

"Should we be afraid?" I asked tentatively.

"Only if you want," the lion answered gently, "but there's no need.

We walked inside the door and were greeted by a big friendly rhinoceros in tropical swim trunks and a Hawaiian shirt.

"Hello children!" Sang Rhino. "Welcome to the island of Opilopy. This is a magical place with all sorts of adventures and life lessons. So on and so forth. So, who is ready for the fun to begin?"

We were all silent

Michelle timidly raised her hand. "Why are we here?"

"I ask myself that everyday." Laughed Rhino. His laughter was contagious. He snapped his fingers, pointed at us, and said, "No sense in wondering though if you have the ability to find the answer. Follow me to your tree fort cabins and get ready for an adventure."

We couldn't wait to see the island so we hurried up the ladders, left our bags in our cabins, and rushed down to the opening in the jungle floor.

"This way young explorers!" bellowed Rhino walking away with a big wave of his arm. We followed him to a clear-cut path with thick foliage on each side. "If you follow along the path, it will lead you to your first challenge of the island. You have to be brave and caring to make it through."

We all thought for a moment then all chimed in that we were up for the challenge.

"Very well then," said Rhino. "Along you go"

As brave as we were trying to be, we held each other's hand and began along the path. We came upon a shimmering pond of the darkest blue. The water started to bubble and turn all the colors of the rainbow. Then an orange and yellow fish rose up from the middle of the pond with water coming out of its mouth like a fountain.

"Hello Hello!" Said the magical fish. "I see it is an adventure that you wish. Well, have no fear, keep each other near, and soon you will find what you hold dear."

"What's our challenge?" Asked Micky.

"A cave with more treasures than you could ever hold and a lost boy who needs a friend's hand to hold."

Then the fish went back down into the water and the pond appeared as when we first approached.

"To the cave we go!" Said the smallest child with a great deal of courage.

Soon we arrived at "The Cave." No one was feeling particularly brave. We knew not to go in without any light, but we didn't have any way to see where we were going. Joe noticed a set of square stones on the side of the cave. Each one with a flat space for a small hand to fit. We all knew what to do. Pressing our hands on the stones, like magic, torch after torch lit up the walls. We made our way in and bravely kept going forward.

Soon we saw our destination. A giant pile of toys and so much candy. We crept closer and heard a voice yell.

"Leave it alone. It's mine. Go away."

We looked up to see an angry little ghost floating above.

"Why are you here little ghost? Asked Markus

"What's it to you?" Rudely replied the ghost.

"Don't you have any friends?" Margo whispered loudly.

"Why would I need friends, when I have all this treasure?" Boasted the ghost.

"Because friends are to share with and help you along." Answered Michelle.

"Humph." Sneered the ghost. "I don't need to be helped. I think I've been doing just fine for some time and sharing with all of you really doesn't seem that great."

"What do we do now?" Jackson wondered out loud.

Several of the children at the same time whispered, "Run!"

Margo looked around at many confused faces. Suddenly, she gathered her courage and climbed up the pile of treasures. She reached high and grabbed the ghost by the hand. She pulled the little ghost close so their faces were very near each other. The little ghost saw in her eyes something he hadn't seen for a very long time. True kindness and friendship.

What we saw next was incredible. The ghost turned into a real person, and floated softly to the ground. We were all amazed.

"I'm real again!" A shaky voice tearfully said.

"What's your name?" I asked.

"It's been so long since anyone called me by my name, I really don't remember." Our new friend said sadly.

We tried all different kinds of names for him but none seemed to work.

"How about Goldie?" I suggested. "Just a nickname for now until you remember your own name."

"I like that!" Grinned Goldie excitedly.

"Do you all really want to be my friends?"

"Of course we do!" Shrieking with joy, we each shook Goldie's hand.

We marched out of the cave, back to the tree forts, and spent much of the night making each other laugh, and telling stories.

It was only the first day in Opilopy and as hilarious Rhino informed us upon arrival, the island is filled with adventures and life lessons. We have so much more to accomplish.